Marty McGee's Space Lab, No Girls Allowed

Martha Alexander

THE DIAL PRESS ⚜ NEW YORK

For Ryan Y.

With special thanks to Dr. Rose Berry

Published by The Dial Press
1 Dag Hammarskjold Plaza
New York, New York 10017

Copyright © 1981 by Martha Alexander
All rights reserved. Manufactured in the U.S.A.
Second Printing / Design by Denise Cronin Neary

Library of Congress Cataloging in Publication Data

Alexander, Martha G.
Marty McGee's space lab, no girls allowed.

Summary: Marty McGee does not like girls—
especially when they break into his space lab.
I. Title.
PZ7.A3777 Mar   [E]   81-2497
ISBN 0-8037-5156-7   AACR2
ISBN 0-8037-5157-5 (lib. bdg.)

The art for each picture consists of a pencil
and wash drawing with two color overlays,
all reproduced as halftone.

Help! Thief! My space helmet is gone.
Rachel! Rachel, where are you?

I did not take your space helmet. I've never *seen* your space helmet. I haven't even been in your room since you put that sign on the door.

Then where could it *be*?

I've been working for weeks on that helmet.
It was almost ready to work—and now it's gone.

Who are you kidding, Marty? Did you really think
you could make a space helmet that could fly?

Look! It's Jenny!

Jenny, come down here right this minute
and bring my space helmet.

Bad girl, Jenny!

This sign on my lab says NO GIRLS ALLOWED—
and that means *little* girls too.

Jenny, what did you do to this thing?
How did you make it work?

Tell me, ~~you little brat~~!

Tell me right this minute!

Well, Smarty-Marty, what good is a space helmet if you can't make it work?

Maybe Jenny will show *me*.
Would you like me to ask her?

Well—I guess so. But hurry up.

Don't rush me, Marty. This may take time.
You'd better wait in your space lab while
I talk to Jenny.

Your musical rattle!
Wait until Marty hears this.

Well, girls, are you ready to show me now?

Sure, Marty—but only if you'll change
that sign on your door.

I don't believe it! A baby rattle!

Too bad you can't go any higher, Marty—
you're just too heavy.

I guess it only works for little girls
like Jenny.